Sophie

and the wonderful picture

Kaye Umansky
Illustrated by Anna Currey

VICTOR GOLLANCZ

LONDON

Sophie Rabbit and Graham Frog
had painted a wonderful picture.

It had taken them all morning,
and they had used up nearly all
the green paint, but Mrs Badger said
it was worth it.

"Look, everyone!" cried Mrs Badger
when she saw it. "Just stop
for a moment, and look at this
lovely painting. What is it, you two?"

"It's the pond where I live," explained Graham. "That's my lily pad there, look. And those green blobs are all my relations. Sophie painted those. Go on Sophie, tell them."

Sophie blushed and shook her head.

"You do it, Graham," she whispered. "You're so much better at explaining things than me."

So Graham explained all about the painting. He did it so well that when he finished, the class clapped.

"Tomorrow, your mums and dads will be coming to see the end of term assembly," said Mrs Badger. "Would you like to show your painting?"

"Yes please," said Graham immediately.

But Sophie wasn't so sure.

"I'm scared of standing up in front of everyone," she confided to Graham. "I'll feel shy. All those eyes staring at me!"

"Don't worry," said Graham. "I'll do all the talking. All you have to do is hold it the right way up."

"Are you coming to assembly tomorrow?" Sophie asked her mum and dad, when she got home.

"Of course, love," said her mum.

"Wild ferrets wouldn't keep me away," said Sophie's dad. "Especially now I know our Soph's the star."

"I'm not doing much," said Sophie. "Just holding up a painting. Graham's doing all the talking. My bit's not at all  important."

But that night, Sophie couldn't get to sleep.

"What's up, Soph?" asked her dad when he came to tuck her in. "Is it stage fright?"

Sophie nodded.

"Suppose I hold it upside down?" she whispered. "What if I drop it?"

"You won't," said George Rabbit.
"But if you do, just keep smiling.
You can get away with most things if
you've got a big smile on your face."

The following morning, the school hall was crammed with everyone's relations.

Sophie's mum and dad arrived early, and sat near the door so that Gareth could be taken out if he played up. Sophie's dad gave her a big wink, and Sophie gave him a timid little wave.

As for Graham's relations – well! They took up the whole front row looking proud enough to burst.

"Good morning, everyone," said
Mrs Badger. "To start our show,
Gordon Fox, Andrew Otter and
Rebecca Water-Rat will do a dance
entitled *Falling Leaves*."

Gordon, Andrew and Rebecca stood up,
Mrs Badger took her place at
the piano, and the show began.

The Falling Leaves danced
beautifully, and got a big clap.

So did Kelly and Fran Mouse,
when they sang their cheese song.

Terry Tortoise showed a fishing rod
he had made, and everyone nodded
and said how clever he was.

Then it was Graham and Sophie's turn.

"Graham and Sophie will now tell you
all about their new picture," said
Mrs Badger.

Sophie's mum and dad craned their necks.

Graham's relations sat up straight, and nudged each other excitedly.

"Stand up, you two. Hold it up high, Sophie, so everyone can see," said Mrs Badger.

Heart in her mouth, Sophie stood up
and held the picture high.

"Come on Graham," she whispered.
"Stand up! It's our turn."

But Graham didn't move.

To everyone's surprise, he just
sat there.

His face looked a paler green than
usual.

He stared miserably at all his
expectant relations. He opened his
mouth, but no sound came out.

Desperately, he rolled his eyes
at Sophie, and shook his head.

"Can't!" he said, in a small,
strangled voice.

It was true. Graham couldn't.

"All right," whispered Sophie.
"You do the holding. I'll do
the talking."

Gratefully, Graham stood up,
took the picture, and held it high.

Sophie caught George Rabbit's eye.
She took a deep breath, gave a
wobbly smile, and began to speak.

"This is a painting we did of
Graham's pond," she said, in a clear
voice. "This is Graham's lily pad, and
this is a mayfly, and these are reeds.

And these are all his relations ..."

And Sophie told the audience all
about the painting, while Graham held
it as high as he possibly could.

When she had finished, there came
a storm of applause.

Graham's relations stood up
and cheered, and so did Sophie's
mum and dad. Even Gareth joined in.

"Thanks, Sophie. I'm sorry about that," whispered Graham. "It was all those eyes, staring at me!"

"I know what you mean," said Sophie, waving at her mum and dad, who were still clapping their paws off.

"You were really good," said Graham. "I thought you said you were shy?"

"I was," said Sophie, her eyes shining. "Once. But not any more."

53 *TM*, p. 19.

54 RLFC3/2/27/128; Distress Papers, 1847 (NAI, D609).

55 RLFC3/2/27/128.

56 Kinealy, *A death dealing Famine*, p. 105.

57 Ibid.

58 *NG*, 14 July 1847; 31 July 1847.

59 Ibid., 31 July 1847; 18 Aug. 1847.

60 Grace, *NPLU*, p. 26.

61 *NG*, 15 Mar. 1845; 9 May 1846; 24 July 1847.

62 Grace, *NPLU*, p. 29; *NG*, 24 June 1848.

63 *NG*, 3 Mar. 1849.

64 Ibid., 14 Apr. 1847; 16 June 1847; 21 July 1847.

65 Grace, *NPLU*, p. 153; *NG*, 14 July 1847; 28 July 1847; 18 Aug. 1847; 2 Oct. 1847.

66 *TM*, p. 22.

67 Nenagh union board of guardian minute books, 23 Sept. 1847 (Tipperary local studies library, 129/A/4) (hereafter BG 129/A/4).

68 *NG*, 16. Oct. 1847.

69 BG 129/A/4, 14 Oct. 1847.

70 *NG*, 16. Oct. 1847; 20 May 1848; 3 June 1848.

71 Ibid., 25 Sept. 1847.

72 BG 129/A/4, 28 Oct. 1847.

73 *NG*, 30 Oct. 1847.

74 TM, p. 28.

75 *NG*, 21 Aug. 1847; 11 Sept. 1847.

76 BG 129/A/4, 28 Oct. 1847.

77 Ibid., 11 Nov. 1847.

78 *NG*, 13 Nov. 1847.

79 Ibid., 17 Nov. 1847.

80 Grace, *NPLU*, p. 116.

81 *NG*, 5 Jan. 1848; 11 Mar. 1848.

82 *NG*, 8 Dec. 1847.

83 Toomevara R.C. baptismal register.

84 *NG*, 8 Dec. 1847; 18 Dec. 1847.

85 BG 129/A/5, 27–29 Jan. 1848.

86 *NG*, 12 Feb. 1848; 19 Feb. 1848; 1 Apr. 1848; 11 Sept. 1848.

87 BG 129/A/5, 26 Feb. 1848.

88 *NG*, 1 Dec. 1847; 6 May. 1848; 3 June 1848; 17 June 1848.

89 Ibid., 5 July 1848.

90 *NG*, 9 Apr. 1848; 15 Apr. 1848; 6 May. 1848; 13 May 1848.

91 Ibid., 9 May 1849.

92 *NG*, 5 Dec. 1846; 8 May. 1847; 11 Mar. 1848; 2 Sept. 1848.

93 BG 129/A/5, 2 Sept. 1848.

94 *NG*, 12 Aug. 1848.

95 *NG*, 15 Jan. 1847; 22 Jan. 1848; 12 Aug. 1848; 28 Oct. 1848.

96 TM, pp 19–22.

97 Interview with Robert J. Powell of Ballinaclough, Nenagh, County Tipperary (19 Sept. 2009).

98 *NG*, 26 Apr. 1848.

99 *TV*, 12 Sept. 1848.

1 I.F.C., 1937–8 (Clash School, Toomevara, p. 105: microfilm, Tipperary local studies library).

2 Kinealy, *A death dealing Famine*, p. 135.

3 *NG*, 3 Jan. 1849; 31 Jan. 1849; 7 Feb. 1849; 10 Feb. 1849; 14 Feb. 1849.

4 Ibid., 12 May 1849.

5 Ibid., 24 Feb. 1849; 14 Apr. 1849; 12 May 1849.

6 *NG*, 7 Apr. 1849.

7 Ibid.

8 TM, p. 20.

9 Marnane, 'Famine in South Tipperary', pt. 4, *THSJ* (1999) pp 16–7.

10 Cole Bowen estate rental records, 1847–48 (In possession of Tipperary local studies library).

11 *NG*, 13 Sept. 1848.

12 Ibid., 10 Mar. 1849; 16 May 1849; 20 May 1848; 24 June 1846; 1 July 1848.

13 Ibid., 30 Aug. 1848; 10 Nov. 1847; 29 Apr. 1848; 5 July 1848.

14 Cole Bowen estate rental records, 1848–9 (In possession of Tipperary local studies library).

3. CLEARANCE

1 *NG*, 20 May 1848.

2 TM, p. 18; *TV*, 26 May 1849; *NG*, 20 May 1849.

3 TM, pp 18–19.

4 *TV*, 30 May 1849; TM, p. 23.

5 TM, p. 23.

6 *NG*, 26 May 1849.

7 *TV*, 26 May 1849.

8 TM, p. 24.

9 *TV*, 26 May 1849.

10 TM, p. 35.

11 *TV*, 26 May 1849; TM, p. 23.

12 Ibid.

13 TM, p. 24.

14 *TV*, 26 May 1849.

15 TM, p. 25.

16 *TV*, 3 May 1849.

17 TM, pp 25–27.

18 *TV*, 26 May 1849.

19 *NG*, 26 May 1849.

20 *TV*, 30 May 1849.

21 *NG*, 2 Jun 1849.

22 *NG*, 26 May 1849.

23 Marnane, 'Famine in South Tipperary', pt. 5 *THSJ* (2000), 73–119.

24 TM, pp 18–26.

25 *TV*, 30 May 1849.

26 *The Times*, 28 May 1849.

27 *TV*, 2 June 1849.

28 *NG*, 26 May 1849.

29 Ibid., 2 Jun 1849.

30 *TV*, 30 May 1849.

31 Ibid., 30 May 1849; 6 June 1849.

32 *NG*, 16 Jun 1849.

33 *TV*, 13 June 1849.

34 Ibid., 16 June 1849.

35 TM, p. 31.

36 *NG*, 20 Jun 1849.

37 *TV*, 30 May 1849.

38 *NG*, 25 Aug. 1849.

39 Kinealy, *This great calamity*, p. 265.

40 Kinealy, *A death dealing Famine*, p. 141.

41 TM, p. 25.

42 TM, p. 26.

43 *NG*, 6 Mar. 1850; TM, p. 33.

44 TM, pp 32–3.

45 *NG*, 6 Mar. 1850.

46 *TV*, 30 May 1849.

47 TM, p. 26.

48 *NG*, 6 Mar. 1850.

49 Ibid.

50 TM, p. 33.

51 Ibid., p. 34.

52 *TV*, 3 May 1849.

53 TM, p. 35.

54 *NG*, 22 May 1850; TM, p. 33.

55 *NG*, 22 May 1850.

56 Ibid., 13 Sept. 1851.

57 Ibid., 4 Dec. 1850; 7 Dec. 1850.

58 TM, p. 35.
59 Interview with William O'Brien Snr. of Mountain Lodge, Toomevara, Co Tipperary (13 June 2009).
60 NG, 21 Feb. 2009.
61 TM, pp 36–8.

4. AFTER THE CLEARANCE

1 TV, 26 May 1849; 30 May 1849.
2 Interview with William O'Brien Snr. of Mountain Lodge, Toomevara, Co. Tipperary (13 June 2009).
3 NG, 29 Aug. 1849.
4 NG, 5 Sept. 1849; 24 Oct. 1849; 3 Nov. 1849; 7 Nov. 1849.
5 NG, 2 Mar. 1850; NG, 15 Mar. 1851.
6 NG, 23 Feb. 1850; 16 Apr. 1851; 7 May 1851; 21 May 1851; 14 June 1851; 24 Apr. 1850; 26 June 1850; 24 July 1850; 12 July 1851.
7 NG, 2 Mar. 1850; NG, 17 Apr. 1850; 26 Apr. 1851.
8 Grace, NPLU, p. 192, 193.
9 NG, 25 June 1851.
10 Ibid., 16 July 1851.
11 Ó Gráda, The great Irish Famine, p. 69.
12 Ó Gráda, Black '47 and beyond, p. 41.
13 1851 census report, pp 288–93, H.C. 1852–3 (1549), xci.649, 670–5; Census of Ireland 1851: part I., Area, population, and

number of houses, by townlands and electoral divisions; part VI., general report, p. 18. H.C. 1856 [2134], xxxi.1, xv. (Hereafter 1851 general census report).
14 Litton, The Irish Famine, p. 130.
15 1851 census report, p. 1671, H.C. 1852–3 (1549), xci.649, 289.
16 1851 census report, pp 288–93, H.C. 1852–3 (1549), xci.649, 670–5.
17 Ibid.
18 Ibid.
19 Griffiths valuation, p. 24.
20 Ó Gráda, Black '47 and beyond, p. 41.
21 Toomevara R.C. baptismal register, 1831–56.
22 Ibid.
23 1851 general census report, p. 23. H.C. 1856 [2134], xxxi.1, xxiii.
24 1851 census report, pp 288–93, H.C. 1852–3 (1549), xci.649, 670–5.
25 Griffith's valuation, pp 1–93 (This calculation excludes four corn and flour mills in the parish as their higher valuation would distort the average valuation).
26 1841 census report, p. 232, 256, H.C. 1843 (504), xxiv.1, 345, 368.
27 Griffith's valuation, pp 1–93.
28 Cathal O'Connell, The state and housing in Ireland: ideology, policy and practice (New York, 2007), p. 4.
29 Marnane, 'Famine in South Tipperary', pt. 5 THSJ (2000), 73–119.

30 Ó Gráda, Black 47 and beyond, p. 125; p. 156.
31 Griffith's valuation, pp 1–93.
32 Ibid.
33 Return by provinces and counties of cases of eviction under knowledge of Royal Irish Constabulary 1849–80, p. 8, H.C. 1881 (185), lxxvii.725 (hereafte Eviction under knowledge of RIC).
34 Eviction under knowledge of RIC, p. 8, H.C. 1881 (185), lxxvii.725.
35 Marnane, 'Famine in South Tipperary', pt. 4, THSJ (1999), 16–17.
36 O.S. Map 25", Tipperary TY02: (1888–1913). © Ordnance Survey Ireland / Government of Ireland, Copyright Permit No. MP 003310
37 Grace, NPLU, p. 189.
38 Ibid., p. 190.
39 Marnane, 'Famine in South Tipperary', pt. 5 THSJ (2000), 73–119.
40 Woodham Smith, The great hunger, p. 412.
41 Donnelly, The great Irish potato Famine, p. 210.
42 Ibid.
43 I.F.C. 1937–8, (Gort an Gharrdha school, Toomevara, Co. Tipperary, p. 320: micro-film, Tipperary local studies Library)
44 NG, 6 Mar. 1850.
45 I.F.C. 1937–8 (Gort an Gharrdha school) p. 320